Hide & Seek

By Il Sung Na

meadowside
CHILDREN'S BOOKS

At the edge of the vast rainforest, where sunlight shines through the leaves, the animals gather together.

Something is about to happen!

'Let's play
hide and seek!'
says Chameleon.

'I'll count!' says Elephant.

'1...'

The animals run and hide.

'Hey!
No peeking!'
shouts Flamingo.

'2...'

'I wonder which tree
I should hide behind?'
says Giraffe.

'3...'

'Can I hide
behind this rock?'
wonders Rhino.

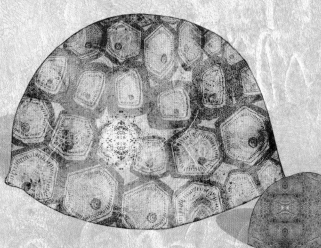

'4...'

'That's my shell!'
whispers Tortoise.

'5…'

'I will pretend
I am a statue,'
says Gorilla very quietly.

'6...'

'**We'll hide up here,**'
flutter the starlings.

"7..."

'And we'll hide down here,'
shuffle the bushbabies.

'8...'

'Quick!

Everybody hide...!'

say the little ones.

'9...'

Elephant's voice
gets louder...

'**10!**'

cries Elephant.

'Ready or not,
here I come!'

Elephant seeks high...

...and low.

'Found
you all!'

'And
found
you!'
he cries.

'But
what about
Chameleon?'
they say.

So, at the edge of the vast rainforest,
where sunlight is fading,
the animals look everywhere
for Chameleon.

'We give up!' they cry.
'Come out, come out,
wherever you are!'

'**Found you!**'
cries Chameleon.

For Sarah, Lucy & Simon

First published in 2011
by Meadowside Children's Books,
185 Fleet Street, London EC4A 2HS
www.meadowsidebooks.com

Text & Illustrations © Il Sung Na 2011

The right of Il Sung Na to be identified
as the author and illustrator of this work
has been asserted by him in accordance
with the Copyright, Designs and Patents Act, 1988

A CIP catalogue record for this book is available
from the British Library
10 9 8 7 6 5 4 3 2 1

Paper used in the production of this book is a natural,
recyclable product from wood grown in sustainable forests

Printed in China